THIS BOOK HAS ALPACAS

I ♥ Alpacas

AND BEARS

David Fickling Books

Scholastic Inc.
New York

Emma Perry AND Rikin Parekh

When he wasn't busy munching grass, Alfonso the alpaca loved nothing more than relaxing with a good story.

But as he looked at everything around him, Alfonso realized something was wrong.

Very wrong . . .

Bears Rule Vol. 1

Be More Bear!

Bear It

DVD

Bears & Power

A Tale of Two Bears

King Bear

Bears Everywhere

CD!

Bears are EVERYWHERE!

Alpacas are . . . NOWHERE!

Bears, bears, bears — cuddly, friendly, grumpy, and hungry — EVERY type of bear! But not a **single** alpaca.

"This is a disaster!" said Alfonso. "We need alpaca stories, and we need them **NOW.** And I'm just the alpaca for the job."

So off he bounced to get started, but . . .

. . . holding a pen with his feet was awkward.

And Alfonso didn't have much luck with his tail . . .

. . . or even his mouth.

"I can't do it,"

said Alfonso as he flopped down onto the grass.

So he decided to visit his friend Colin. A bear.

"Hi, Colin. Let's write a
fantastic story about
alpacas," said Alfonso.
"Not now," said Colin.
"I'm busy."

"But why are
bears always
in stories?"
asked Alfonso.
"It's not fair!"

"We're cute, charming, and clever.
Everyone loves bears!" said Colin.

Alfonso was cute, charming,
and clever too.

But could he convince
Colin to help him write
a story about alpacas?

Yes! Yes!

Yes!

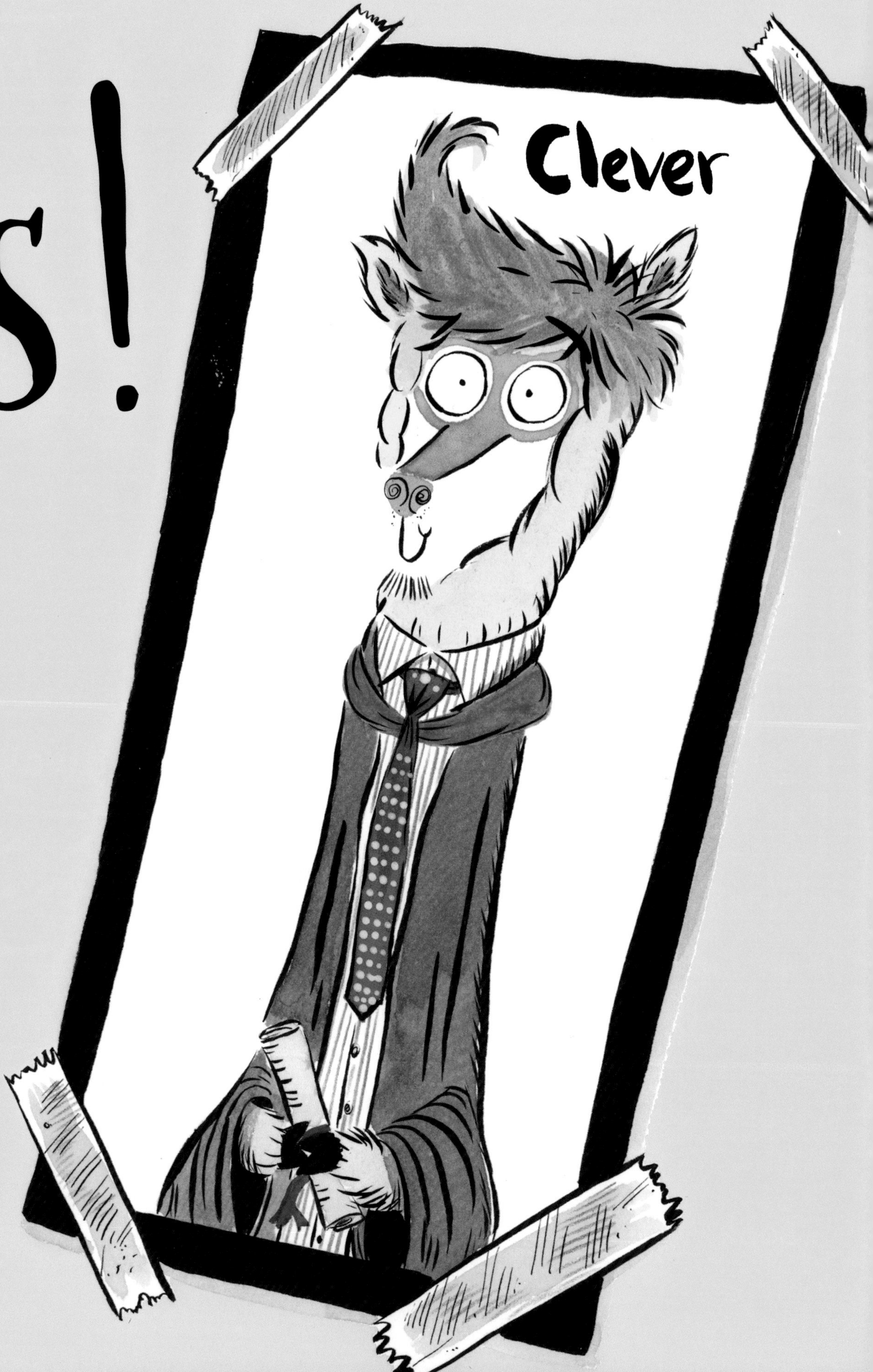

MONDAY

at Colin's yoga class

"Colin, we need to write a book about an alpaca," said Alfonso.

"Nope," said Colin.

TUESDAY

in Colin's bath cave

"Ooooh, Colin, a relaxing bath — I bet you're thinking up ideas for our alpaca book," said Alfonso.

"We'd make a perfect team," said Alfonso.
"No!" said Colin.
"But why?" asked Alfonso.

"Because alpacas are **noisy, clumsy, careless,**
and **REALLY annoying.**"

"OH!" Alfonso's big smile melted away . . .

But then
he realized
something
very
important . . .

. . . Colin was WRONG!

"Alpacas ARE
GREAT!"

And Alfonso
decided to prove
just how
great alpacas
really are . . .

So he pulled on his dancing shoes, then shimmied around the field, before pulling a delightfully fluffy rabbit out from beneath his floppy fringe!

He stood on his head while humming five nursery rhymes — backward.

He gobbled five gigantic grass pies in less than five minutes.

He showed off his skateboarding skills.

Then he strummed
on his electric guitar.

And for his **grand finale . . .**

Alfonso performed the four-legged splits in MIDAIR!

Colin couldn't believe his eyes.

"I'm sorry," said Colin. "I was wrong. You're not **noisy, clumsy, careless,** or **annoying**. Well, not *all* the time!

"Alfonso, you SHOULD be in a story and YOU can make it happen. If you need help, I'm right here."

"Woo-hoo!

I knew you'd see it my way . . .
eventually. It's going to be
the best story **EVER!**"
said Alfonso.

1 WRITING

2 SHARING

3 REWRITING AND CORRECTING

4 DRAWING AND COLORING

⑤ FINAL CHECKS

⑥ PRINTING

Ta-da! Finished story!

"This book is

FABULOUS!"

said Colin.

"I know!"
said Alfonso.
"And the **best**
thing is, this
is only the
beginning.

Have you ever noticed
that bears are absolutely

EVERYWHERE?

Alfonso the alpaca has and
it really gets on his last nerve!

He's decided that alpacas
should get the recognition
(AND LOVE!) that they deserve.
And sometimes it only takes one voice
spea—— to make a change.

It's t————— d—

"I've got plans, Colin . . ."

"... GREAT PLANS," announced Alfonso. "Check out the full **Alfonso**™ line, available absolutely EVERYWHERE!"

AMAZING ALPACA FACTS

Alpacas come from South America.

There are two types of alpaca – suri (with long, dreadlock-style wool) and huacaya (with thick, crimped wool like a teddy bear).

Alpacas are the smallest members of the camel family.

Boing!

They are great at bouncing!

AMAZING ALPACA FACTS

Their babies are called cria and they come in twenty-two different colors!

Cria (Baby Alpaca)

Their wool is sooo soft – not even a teeny bit itchy. *And* it is water-resistant.

They are great at humming!

Alpacas LOVE a good dust bath.

To Leisa – for championing, cheering & encouraging Alfonso's antics. Thank you xxx E. P.

For Dada and Bella xx R. P.

WARNING: THIS BOOK WILL MAKE YOU ALPACA-MAD!
Text copyright © 2020 by Emma Perry
Illustrations copyright © 2020 by Rikin Parekh

First published in the United Kingdom in 2020 by David Fickling Books, 31 Beaumont Street, Oxford OX1 2NP. • *www.davidficklingbooks.com*

ISBN 978-1-338-63570-6
10 9 8 7 6 5 4 3 2 1   21 22 23 24 25

Printed in the U.S.A. 141
First printing January 2021

Book design by Keight Bergmann